AMAZING SUPER SIMPLE INVENTIONS

SUPER SIMPLE

AIRCRAFT
PROJECTS

INSPIRING & EDUCATIONAL
SCIENCE ACTIVITIES

ALEX KUSKOWSKI

Consulting Editor, Diane Craig, M.A./Reading Specialist

Super Sandcastle

An Imprint of Abdo Publishing
abdopublishing.com

abdopublishing.com

Published by Abdo Publishing, a division of ABDO, PO Box 398166, Minneapolis, Minnesota 55439. Copyright © 2016 by Abdo Consulting Group, Inc. International copyrights reserved in all countries. No part of this book may be reproduced in any form without written permission from the publisher. Super SandCastle™ is a trademark and logo of Abdo Publishing.

Printed in the United States of America, North Mankato, Minnesota
062015
092015

THIS BOOK CONTAINS
RECYCLED MATERIALS

Editor: Liz Salzmann
Content Developer: Nancy Tuminelly
Cover and Interior Design and Production: Mighty Media, Inc.
Photo Credits: Library of Congress, Mighty Media, Inc.,
Shutterstock, US Air Force, Wikicommons

The following manufacturers/names appearing in this book are trademarks: 3M™
Scotch®, CraftSmart®, Sharpie®

Library of Congress Cataloging-in-Publication Data

Kuskowski, Alex, author.
  Super simple aircraft projects : inspiring & educational science activities / Alex Kuskowski ; consulting editor, Diane Craig, M.A./Reading specialist.
    pages cm -- (Amazing super simple inventions)
  Audience: K to grade 4.
  ISBN 978-1-62403-728-3
1. Aeronautics--Experiments--Juvenile literature. 2. Airplanes--History--Juvenile literature. 3. Flying-machines--Models--Juvenile literature. 4. Wright, Orville, 1871-1948--Juvenile literature. 5. Wright, Wilbur, 1867-1912--Juvenile literature. I. Craig, Diane, editor. II. Title. III. Series: Kuskowski, Alex. Amazing super simple inventions.
  TL547.K87 2016
  629.130078--dc23

                        2014049929

Super SandCastle™ books are created by a team of professional educators, reading specialists, and content developers around five essential components—phonemic awareness, phonics, vocabulary, text comprehension, and fluency—to assist young readers as they develop reading skills and strategies and increase their general knowledge. All books are written, reviewed, and leveled for guided reading and early reading intervention programs for use in shared, guided, and independent reading and writing activities to support a balanced approach to literacy instruction.

To Adult Helpers

The projects in this title are fun and simple. There are just a few things to remember to keep kids safe. Some projects require the use of sharp or hot objects. Also, kids may be using messy materials such as glue or paint. Make sure they protect their clothes and work surfaces. Review the projects before starting, and be ready to assist when necessary.

KEY SYMBOLS

Watch for these warning symbols in this book. Here is what they mean.

HOT!
You will be working with something hot. Get help!

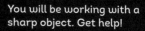
SHARP!
You will be working with a sharp object. Get help!

CONTENTS

AIRCRAFT

AN INTRODUCTION

Look up! There are all sorts of machines flying through the air. Learn what carries people through the sky. Read more about aircraft, from the first hot air balloon flight to today's jet airplanes.

Many people worked to make human flight happen. Find out how today's flying machines work. Discover the invention of flight for yourself!

TYPES OF AIRCRAFT

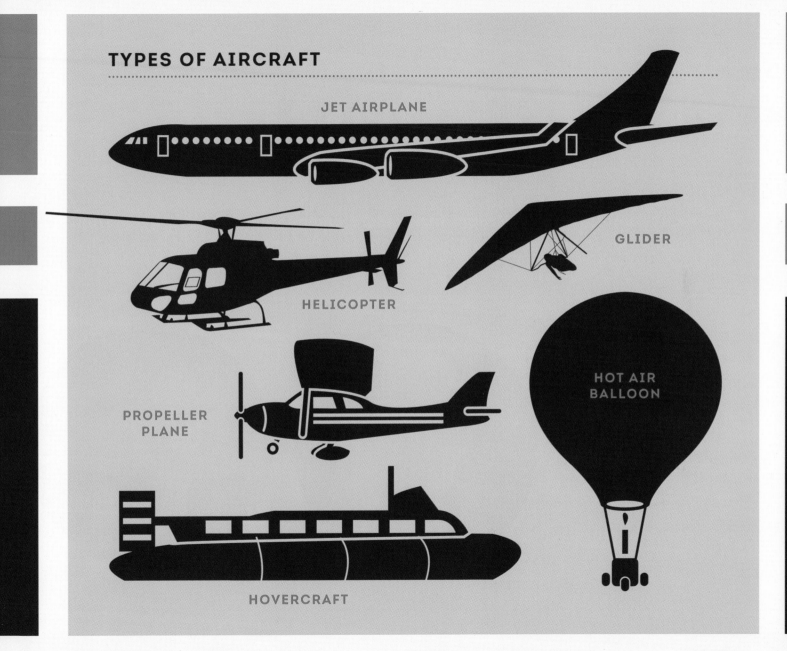

JET AIRPLANE

HELICOPTER

GLIDER

PROPELLER PLANE

HOT AIR BALLOON

HOVERCRAFT

WRIGHT BROTHERS

The most famous of all the flight **innovators** were the Wright brothers. They spent their lives **researching** flight. Then they taught the world how to fly.

The brothers worked for years perfecting flying machines. They moved to windy Kitty Hawk, North Carolina, to test their ideas on flight.

WILBUR WRIGHT

ORVILLE WRIGHT

OTHER IMPORTANT PEOPLE

Jean-François Pilâtre de Rozier and François Laurent d'Arlandes. They were the first to fly in a hot air balloon.

Otto Lilienthal. The "King of Gliders" inspired many to take flight.

Charles A. Lindbergh. The first man to fly across the Atlantic Ocean.

Amelia Earhart. The first woman to fly across the Atlantic Ocean.

Many days they would go out and test flying machines and make notes.

In 1903, they made the first powered flight! It lasted less than one minute, but it was the beginning of air travel.

THEN TO NOW

A TIMELINE OF AIRCRAFT

Henri Giffard's steam-powered airship made its first flight.

Orville and Wilbur Wright made the first powered, controlled flight in an airplane.

Jean-François Pilâtre de Rozier and Marquis d'Arlandes flew in a hot air balloon.

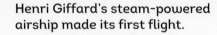

1783   **1797** **1809**   **1852**   **1903** **1907**

André-Jacques Garnerin **parachuted** from a hot air balloon.

George Cayley publishes *On Aerial Navigation*. This is his glider.

The first helicopter lifted a **pilot** off the ground.

Amelia Earhart was the first woman to fly solo across the Atlantic Ocean.

A hovercraft crossed the English Channel.

Charles A. Lindbergh made the first solo flight across the Atlantic Ocean.

1927   **1930**   **1932**   **1947**   **1959**   **1961**

The jet engine was invented.

Charles E. Yeager flew a Bell X-1. He flew faster than the speed of sound.

First manned space flight.

BE AN INVENTOR

LEARN HOW TO THINK LIKE AN INVENTOR!

Inventors have a special way of working. It is a series of steps called the Scientific Method. Follow the steps to work like an inventor.

THE SCIENTIFIC METHOD

1. QUESTION

What question are you trying to answer? Write down the question.

2. GUESS

Try to guess the answer to your question. Write down your guess.

3. EXPERIMENT

Think of a way to find the answer. Write down the steps.

KEEP TRACK

There's another way to be just like an inventor. Inventors make notes about everything they do. So get a notebook. When you do an experiment, write down what happens in each step. It's super simple!

4. MATERIALS

What supplies will you need? Make a list.

5. ANALYSIS

Do the experiment. What happened? Write down the results.

6. CONCLUSION

Was your guess correct? Why or why not?

MATERIALS

acrylic paint

balloons

clear tape

colored construction paper

electric fan

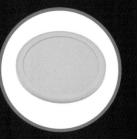

foam paintbrush

golf tees

hot glue gun & glue sticks

masking tape

paper clips

plastic tub lid

pliers

Here are some of the **materials** that you will need.

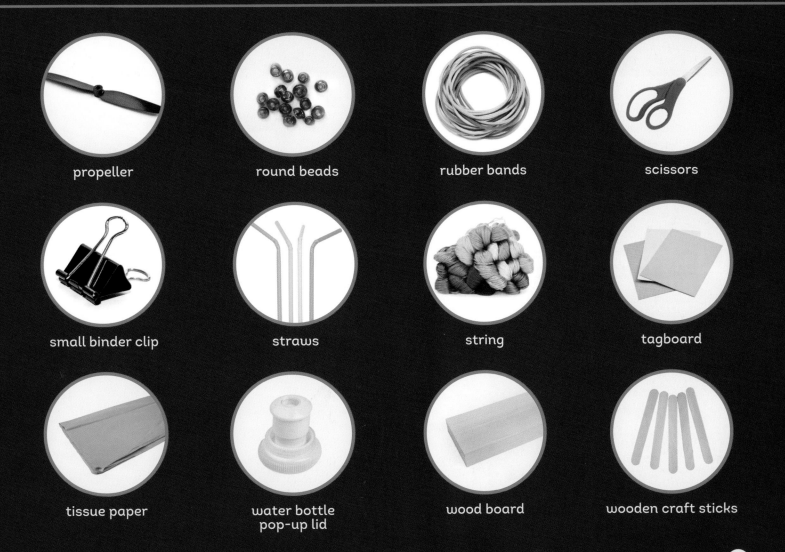

propeller

round beads

rubber bands

scissors

small binder clip

straws

string

tagboard

tissue paper

water bottle pop-up lid

wood board

wooden craft sticks

HELICOPTER

Get your spin on!

MATERIALS: 2 paper clips, wooden craft stick, masking tape, square bead, hot glue gun & glue sticks, colored construction paper, pencil, scissors, pliers, propeller, round bead, rubber band

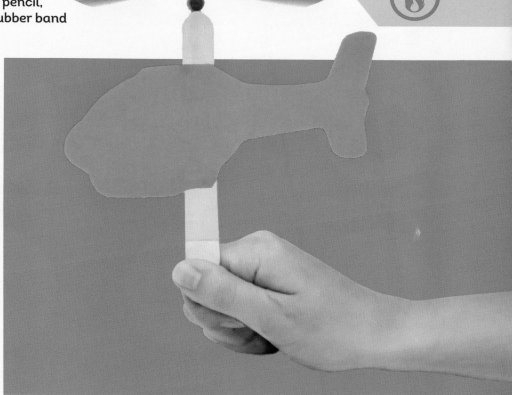

H elicopter **propellers** rotate. The movement creates lift. It pulls the aircraft off the ground. Helicopters use **batteries** to make the propellers rotate.

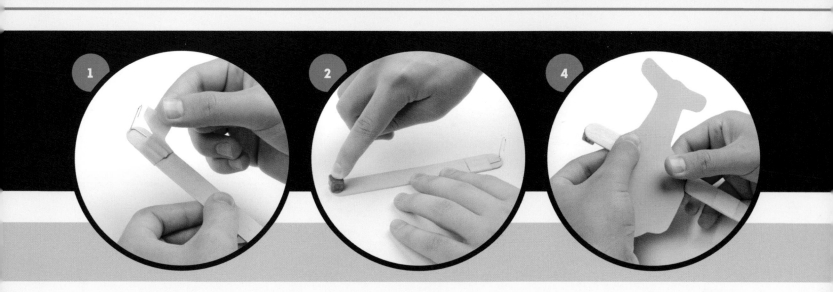

MAKE A HELICOPTER

① Pull the center of a paper clip up. Make an L shape with the paper clip. Hold one end of the paper clip against the end of a craft stick. Tape the paper clip to the craft stick.

② Hot glue the square bead to the other end of the craft stick. The hole should face the end of the stick.

③ Draw a helicopter shape on construction paper. Cut it out.

④ Hot glue the helicopter shape to the craft stick. Leave 1 inch (2.5 cm) of the craft stick above the helicopter. The bead end should be above the helicopter.

continued on next page

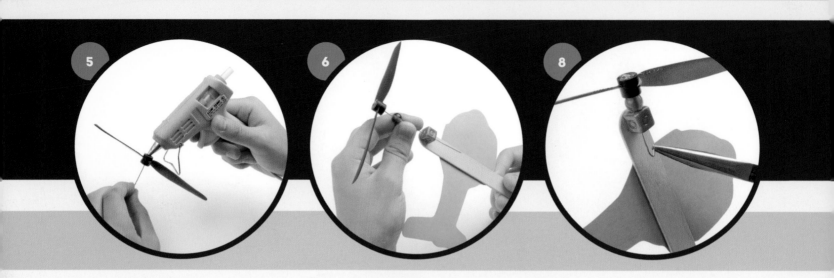

MAKE A HELICOPTER (CONTINUED)

⑤ Straighten a paper clip with the pliers. Bend ¼ inch (.6 cm) of one end to the side. Push the other end of the paper clip through the **propeller**. Pull it until the bent end catches. Hot glue the paper clip to the propeller. Let it dry.

⑥ Put a round bead on the paper clip. Put the wire through the square bead with the propeller on top.

⑦ Measure 1 inch (2.5 cm) of the paper clip below the square bead. Use the pliers to cut the paper clip.

⑧ Use the pliers to bend the end into a small hook.

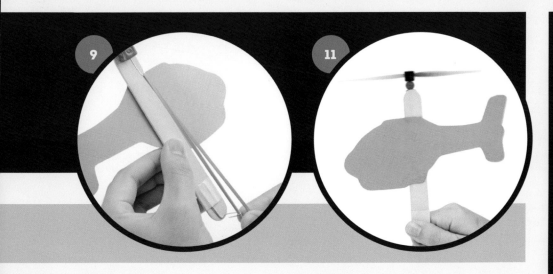

9 Stretch the rubber band between the two paper clips.

10 Hold the craft stick straight up and down. Wind the **propeller** by turning the blades in a full circle. Wind it about 60 times.

11 Let go of the propeller first. Then quickly let go of the craft stick.

12 Try winding the rubber band more than 60 times. Try using shorter and longer rubber bands. See if there's a difference in flight.

HOW DOES IT WORK?

The propeller uses stored energy to make the helicopter move. The wound-up rubber band holds energy. When you let go of the propeller, the rubber band unwinds. It makes the propeller move. The helicopter flies!

CATAPULT PLANE

Fly high with this fun experiment!

MATERIALS: decorative paper, paper clip, safety pin, ruler, clear tape, stapler, hot glue gun & glue sticks, 2 golf tees, board, rubber band

Thrust is important for flight. Airplanes get thrust from motors. You make the thrust for this airplane.

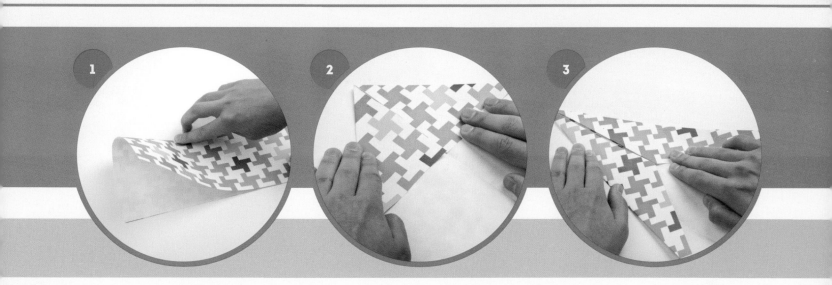

MAKE A CATAPULT PLANE

1 Fold the paper in half **lengthwise**. **Crease** it firmly. Unfold the paper.

2 Fold one corner to the center fold. Fold the opposite corner to the center fold. Crease them firmly.

3 Fold the new corners created by the folds in step 2 to the center. Line the folded sides up with the center fold.

4 Refold the paper along the center fold. The folded corners should be on the inside. Crease it firmly.

continued on next page

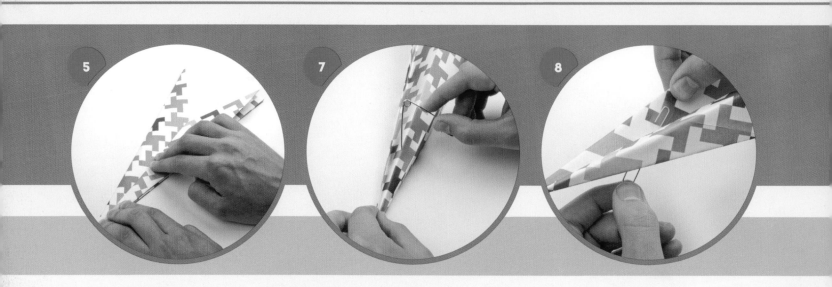

MAKE A CATAPULT PLANE (CONTINUED)

5 Fold one side back. Line it up with the center fold. **Crease** it firmly. Turn the plane over. Fold the other side back the same way.

6 Pull up the center hook of a paper clip. Unfold it until it is one flat piece.

7 Use a safety pin to poke a hole through the center fold. Make the hole 3 inches (7.5 cm) from the front of the plane.

8 Thread the small half of the paper clip up through the hole. Face the hook of the clip toward the front of the plane. Tape the paper clip between the wings.

9 Staple the sides of the plane together. Put the staple under the wings.

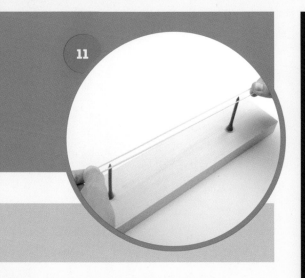

11

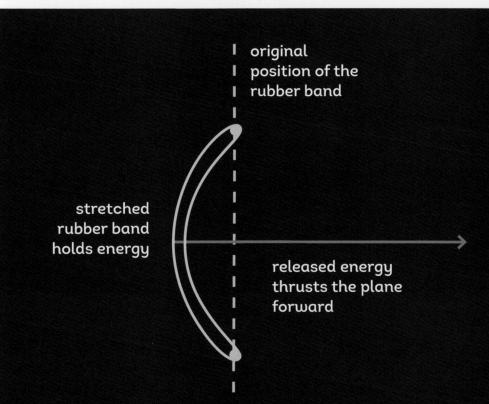

original position of the rubber band

stretched rubber band holds energy

released energy thrusts the plane forward

(10) Hot glue the top of each golf tee to a board. Space the tees 7 inches (18 cm) apart. Let the glue dry.

(11) Stretch a rubber band between the tees. Hook the paper clip under the plane over the rubber band. Pull back on the plane. Let go and watch it fly!

HOW DOES IT WORK?

The **catapult** plane gets thrust from the rubber band. The rubber band holds the energy when you pull the plane back. When you let go, it thrusts the plane forward.

STRAW ROCKET

Shoot your rocket into space!

MATERIALS: decorative paper, ruler, scissors, clear tape, straw, craft glue, duct tape

People use rockets to fly to space and to the moon. Rockets need thrust to fly. They have fuel that is lit on fire. The energy from the fire thrusts the rocket into space.

HOW DOES IT WORK?

The rocket you built uses air from your lungs. By blowing in the straw, you push air through the rocket. It thrusts the rocket up in the air.

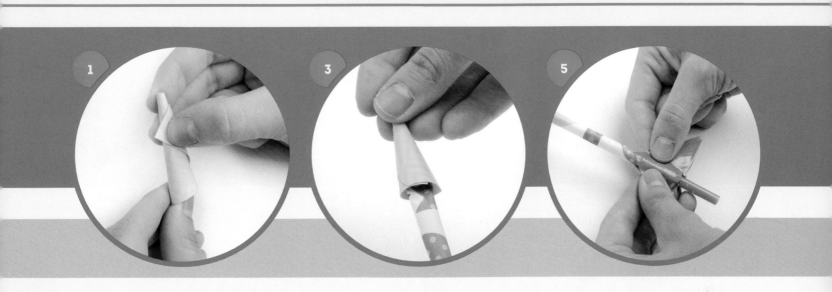

MAKE A STRAW ROCKET

① Cut a 2-inch (5 cm) paper square. Roll it into a cone. Tape the end down. Trim the cone to 1½ (4 cm) inches long.

② Cut out a paper rectangle. Make it 7 inches (18 cm) by 1½ inches (4 cm). Put glue on one long side. Lay a straw on the opposite side. Roll the straw up in the paper. Let the glue dry.

③ Pinch one end of the paper tube. Glue it shut. Glue the cone over the pinched end.

④ Cut a 2-inch (5 cm) square of duct tape. Draw an X in the center of the square. Cut along the lines.

⑤ Push the straw through the hole in the tape. Fold opposite corners of the tape together over the rocket. Do not tape the rocket to the straw.

⑥ Blow on the straw.

HOVERCRAFT

Get off the ground with a hovercraft!

MATERIALS: plastic tub lid, ruler, pen, X-Acto knife, acrylic paint, foam paintbrush, stickers, water bottle pop-up lid, hot glue gun & glue sticks, balloon

Hovercraft are machines that float. They use air to push themselves up. They hover above the ground. Some people think hovercraft will be the **future** of air travel.

HOW DOES IT WORK?

The hovercraft floats using air. The balloon pushes air out under the lid. The lid floats. It will glide across a flat surface.

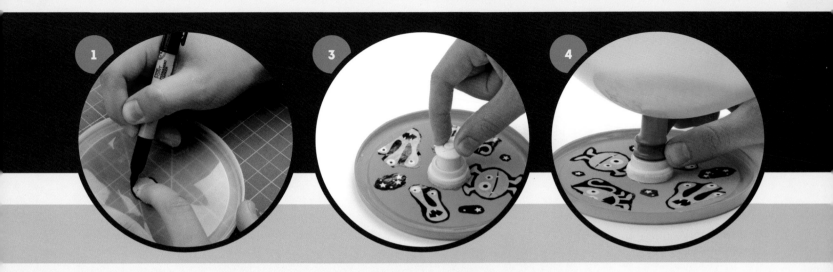

MAKE A HOVERCRAFT

① Draw a ¾-inch (2 cm) circle in the center of a plastic tub lid. Use an X-Acto knife to cut the circle out.

② Paint the lid. Let it dry. Paint on a second coat if necessary. Decorate the lid with stickers.

③ Cover the hole in the lid with the pop-up lid. Hot glue the pop-up lid in place. Let it dry.

④ Blow up the balloon. Pinch the end so the air cannot escape. Close the pop-up lid. Stretch the balloon around the pop-up lid.

⑤ Open the pop-up lid. See how long the balloon hovers.

PERFECT PLANE

Make the perfect paper plane to learn more about flight!

MATERIALS: sheet of paper, ruler, pencil, small binder clip

Paper planes have a lot of lift. If you throw one, it will get a lot of thrust too. Learn how to slow down a fast plane.

HOW DOES IT WORK?

Throwing this paper plane gives it thrust. It is folded to have a lot of lift. The binder clip makes it heavier. This brings the plane down faster.

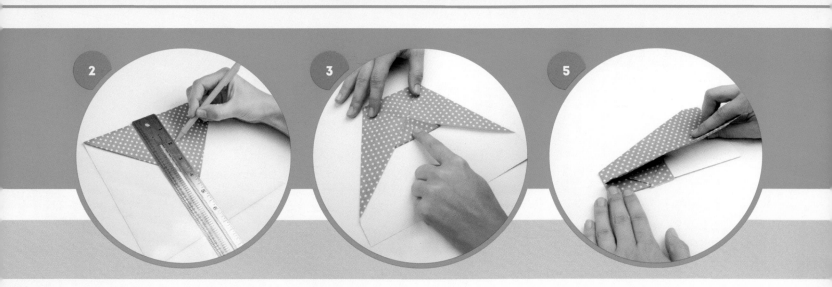

MAKE A PERFECT PLANE

① Fold the paper in half **lengthwise**. **Crease** it firmly. Unfold the paper. Fold two corners to the center. Make a triangle.

② Fold the triangle down. Make a mark on the center fold 2 inches (5 cm) from the top edge.

③ Fold the new top corners to the mark. Fold the point of the triangle up.

④ Turn the plane over. Fold it in half on the center fold.

⑤ Fold one side back. Line it up with the center fold. Crease it firmly. Turn the plane over. Fold the other side back the same way.

⑥ Throw the plane. **Attach** a small binder clip to the bottom. Throw the plane again.

SQUARE KITE

Learn about flight like the Wright brothers!

MATERIALS: tagboard, ruler, pen, scissors, clear tape, tissue paper, string, electric fan

The Wright brothers tested their ideas by making kites! They flew them and studied how the wind affected them.

HOW DOES IT WORK?

The air from the fan lifts the kite. It also creates drag. It pushes the kite in the direction the air is going.

MAKE A SQUARE KITE

① Draw a rectangle on tagboard. Make it 3 inches (7.5 cm) by 12½ inches (31.5 cm). Cut out the rectangle.

② **Crease** the rectangle every 3 inches (7.5 cm). Put a piece of tape on the ½-inch (1.5 cm) tab. Tape it under the other end of the rectangle. It should make a square.

③ Cut thin strips of tissue paper. Tape the strips to the kite.

④ Cut two pieces of string 45 inches (114 cm) long. Tape them to the other side of the kite. Put them in opposite corners. Tie the strings together 4 inches (10 cm) from the kite.

⑤ Turn on the fan. Hold onto the strings. Let the fan blow on the kite.

CONCLUSION

Aircraft such as airplanes and helicopters fly every day. They are everywhere, but do you know how they really work? This book is the first step in discovering what makes aircraft fly. There is a lot more to find out.

Discover more about flight. Look online or at the library. Think of aircraft experiments you can do on your own.

Put on your scientist thinking cap and go on a learning journey!

QUIZ

(1) When did the Wright brothers make the first powered, controlled flight in an airplane?

(2) Name the four principles of flight.

(3) The Wright brothers used kites to test their ideas about flight. **TRUE OR FALSE?**

THINK ABOUT IT!

How has flight changed the world?

Answers: 1. 1903 2. Lift, weight, drag, thrust 3. True

GLOSSARY

attach – to join or connect.

battery – a small container filled with chemicals that makes electrical power.

catapult – a machine used to throw things.

crease – to make a sharp line in something by folding it.

future – the time that hasn't happened yet.

innovator – someone who does something in a new way.

lengthwise – in the direction of the longest side.

material – something needed to make or build something else.

parachute – to jump out of an aircraft and use a large piece of cloth to fall slowly to the ground.

pilot – a person who operates an aircraft or a ship.

propeller – a device with turning blades used to move a vehicle such as an airplane or a boat.

research – to find out more about something.